TRICKY JOURNEYS™ #2

TRICKY RABBIT TALES

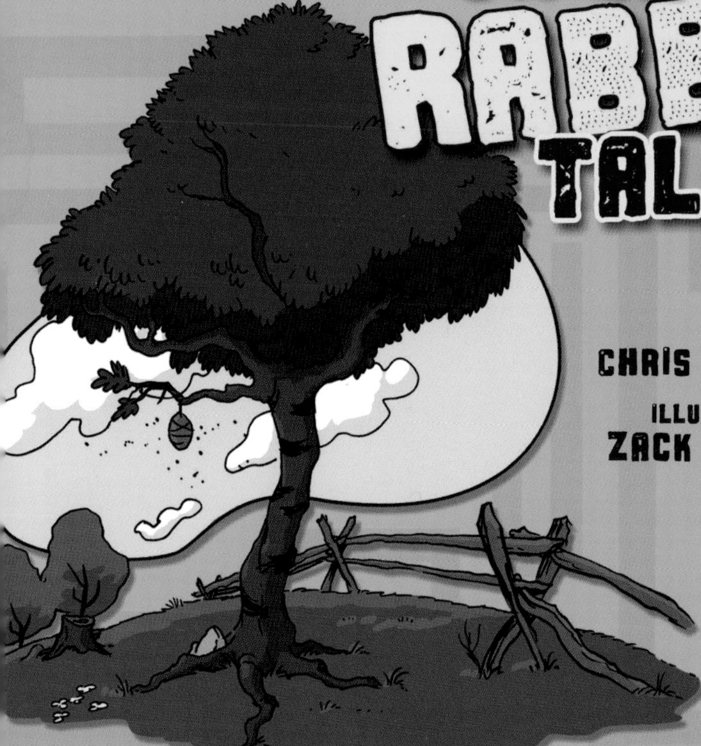

CHRIS SCHWEIZER

ILLUSTRATED BY
ZACK GIALLONGO

GRAPHIC UNIVERSE™ • MINNEAPOLIS • NEW YORK

Story by Chris Schweizer

Illustrations by Zack Giallongo

Coloring by John Novak

Lettering by Grace Lu

Graphic Universe™
A division of Lerner Publishing Group, Inc.
241 First Avenue North
Minneapolis, MN 55401 U.S.A.

Website address: www.lernerbooks.com

Main body text set in CC Dave Gibbons Lower 14/22.
Typeface provided by Comicraft/Active Images.

Library of Congress Cataloging-in-Publication Data

Schweizer, Chris.
    Tricky Rabbit tales / by Chris Schweizer ; illustrated by Zack Giallongo.
        p. cm. — (Tricky journeys)
    Summary: Rabbit sets out to prove he is the cleverest animal of all by playing a truly amazing trick, and the reader helps him make choices as he encounters many other creatures, some friendly and some dangerous.
    ISBN: 978–0–7613–6607–2 (lib. bdg. : alk. paper)
    1. Plot-your-own stories. 2. Graphic novels. [1. Graphic novels. 2. Rabbit (Legendary character)—Fiction. 3. Tricksters—Fiction. 4. Animals—Fiction. 5. Plot-your-own stories.] I. Giallongo, Zack, ill. II. Title.
PZ7.7.S39Trh 2011
741.5'973—dc22   2010049799

Manufactured in the United States of America
1 – CG – 7/15/11

Are you ready for your Tricky Journeys™? You'll find yourself right smack in the middle of this story's tricks, jokes, thrills, and fun.

Each page tells what happens to Rabbit and his friends. **YOU** get to decide what happens next. Read each page until you reach a choice. Then pick the choice **YOU** like best.

But be careful . . . one wrong choice could land Rabbit in a mess even he can't trick his way out of!

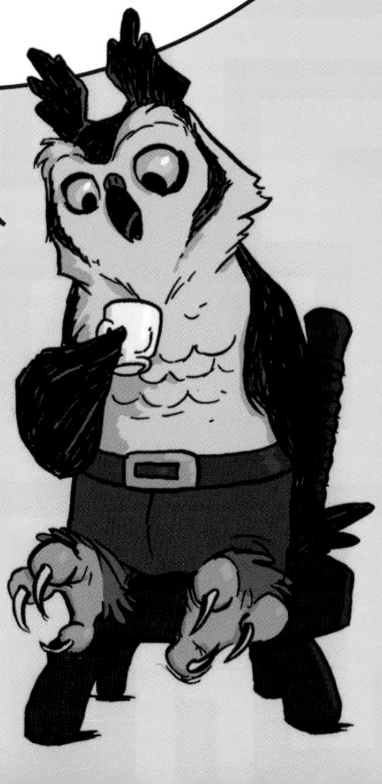

Rabbit hears his neighbor Fox sneaking up behind him. Fox isn't the nicest neighbor. He never cuts his grass...and he's always trying to eat Rabbit.

Rabbit spins around and looks Fox in the eye. "Who are you sneaking up on, Brother Fox?" asks Rabbit. Where Rabbit lives, it's polite for animals to call one another Brother or Sister, even when one of them is trying to eat you.

"Sneaking?" says Fox, looking sneaky. "I wasn't sneaking! I came to tell you the news!"

4 Go on to the next page.
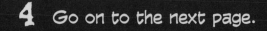

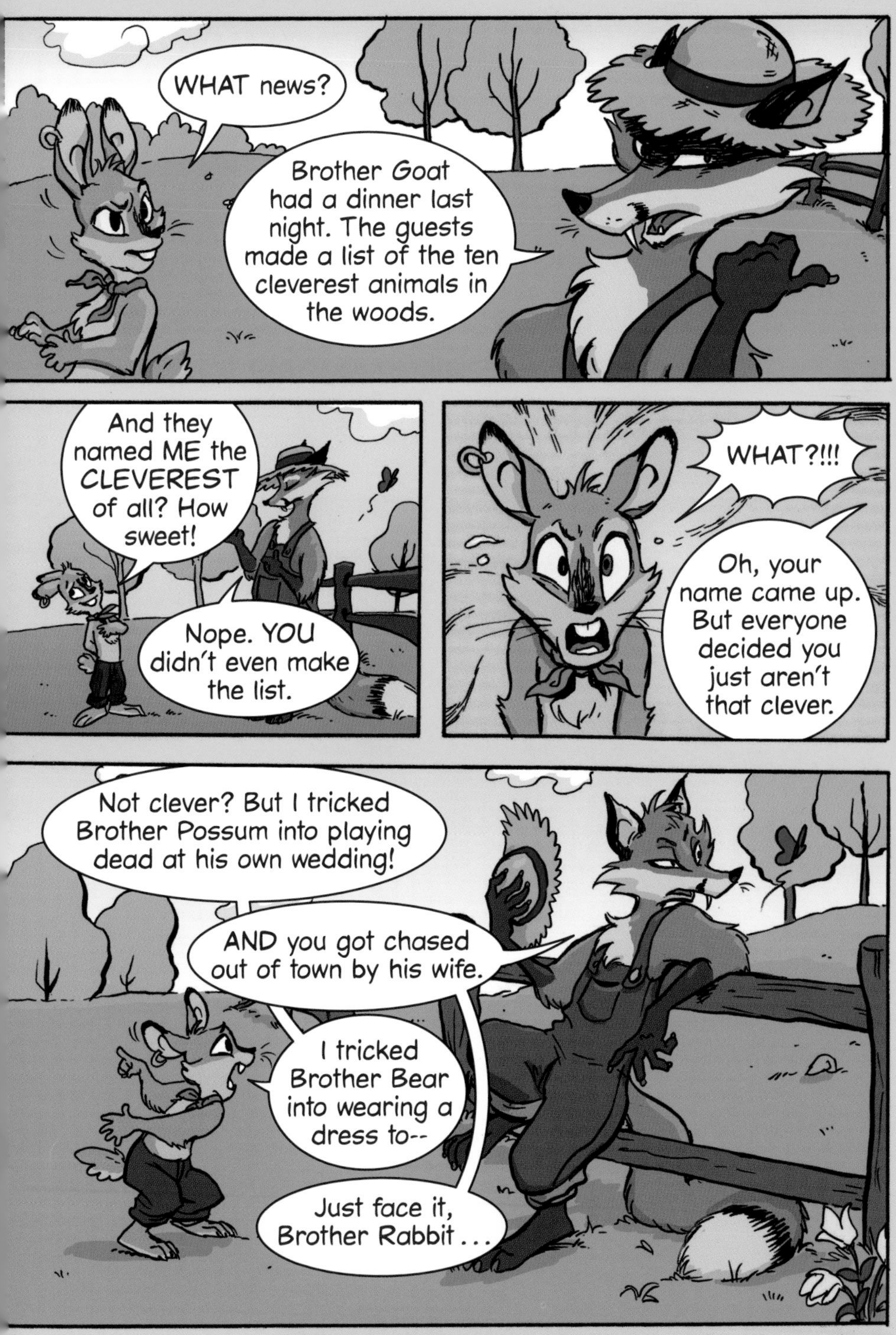

WHAT news?
Brother Goat had a dinner last night. The guests made a list of the ten cleverest animals in the woods.
And they named ME the CLEVEREST of all? How sweet!
Nope. YOU didn't even make the list.
WHAT?!!!
Oh, your name came up. But everyone decided you just aren't that clever.
Not clever? But I tricked Brother Possum into playing dead at his own wedding!
AND you got chased out of town by his wife.
I tricked Brother Bear into wearing a dress to--
Just face it, Brother Rabbit . . .

"...you may play good tricks. But if you were really clever, you wouldn't get caught."

Rabbit can't believe his ears. He's worked hard to make everyone in the woods laugh at his tricks. Maybe he can play a truly amazing trick. Then everyone will agree that he is the cleverest animal of all!

If Rabbit decides to play a trick on the animals who went to Goat's dinner party,

TURN TO PAGE 46.

If Rabbit decides to play a trick on Fox,

TURN TO PAGE 30.

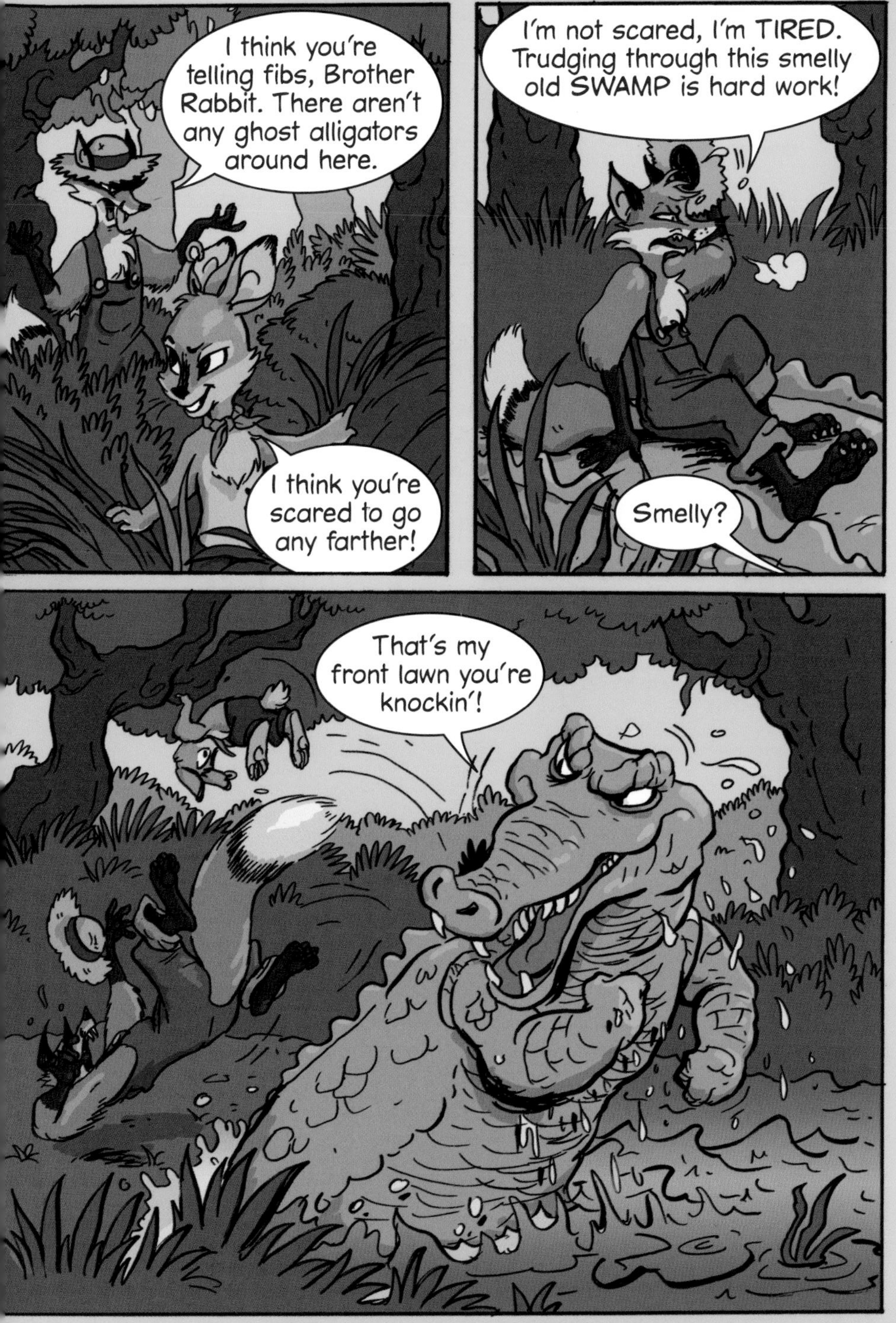
I think you're telling fibs, Brother Rabbit. There aren't any ghost alligators around here.
I think you're scared to go any farther!
I'm not scared, I'm TIRED. Trudging through this smelly old SWAMP is hard work!
Smelly?
That's my front lawn you're knockin'!

Go on to the next page.

"I don't take kindly to folks insulting my home," says the alligator, "so I'm going to eat you up good! Only question is, which one of you should I snack on first?"

If Rabbit tells the alligator to eat Fox,

TURN TO PAGE
55.

If Rabbit tries to trick the gator into not eating either of them,

TURN TO PAGE
24.

"I heard Granny Fox and Granny Rabbit talking the other day," says Rabbit. "Granny Rabbit was so happy that I always bring her fresh honey. Your grandmother was sad. You never bring her honey."

"Well, I didn't know Granny Fox liked honey," says Fox, scratching his chin.

"Oh, she does!" exclaims Rabbit. "And I know where we can get some!" Rabbit smiles. He's going to make Fox look foolish—and make himself look clever. But Fox is crafty. Rabbit had better be careful!

Go on to the next page.

"I don't know if I trust you, Brother Rabbit," says Fox. "You're a tricky one."

"Oh, you can trust me," says Rabbit, holding back a chuckle.

If Rabbit tells Fox that they should make a trade with a honey merchant,

TURN TO PAGE 27.

If Rabbit tells Fox that they should get fresh honey from a beehive,

TURN TO PAGE 62.

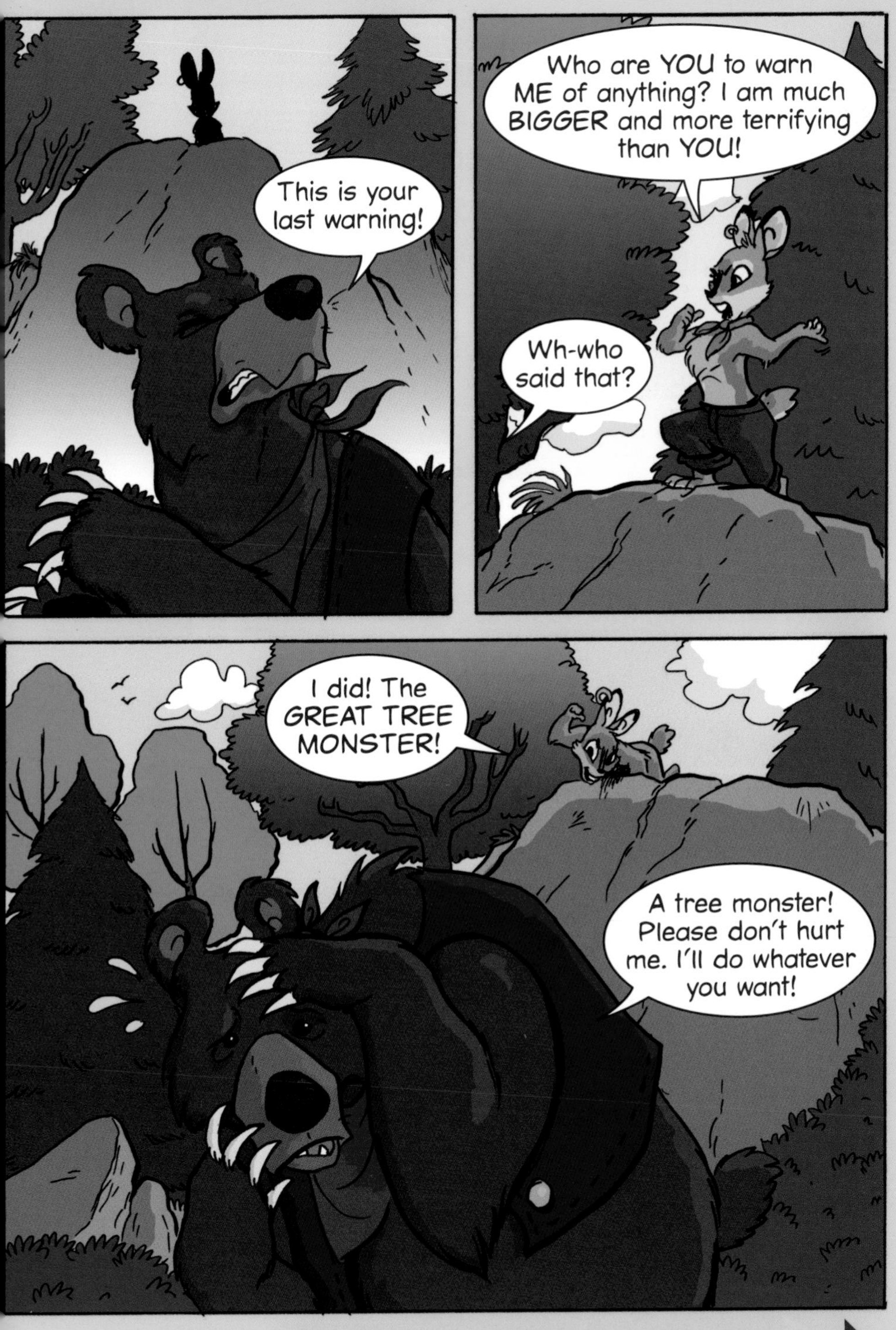
This is your last warning!
Who are YOU to warn ME of anything? I am much BIGGER and more terrifying than YOU!
Wh-who said that?
I did! The GREAT TREE MONSTER!
A tree monster! Please don't hurt me. I'll do whatever you want!

Go on to the next page.

Rabbit has never seen Bear scared. Maybe Rabbit can use this to make Bear do what he wants!

If Rabbit asks Bear to help him find Buck's old antlers,

TURN TO PAGE 51.

If Rabbit demands that Bear give him all of his snacks,

TURN TO PAGE 33.

"I'll race him," says Fox. "I can't lose!"

"You know, you're right!" says Rabbit, suddenly acting very friendly. "This turtle could never beat you. But if he does—which he won't, of course—then you have to admit to everybody that I'm the most clever."

Fox looks at Rabbit suspiciously. "You trickster!" he says. "You're plotting something! You WANT me to race the turtle. Well, I don't care if people think I'm slow. I won't race him!"

As Fox stomps off, Rabbit laughs and laughs. Fox doesn't know that he's already been tricked!

THE END

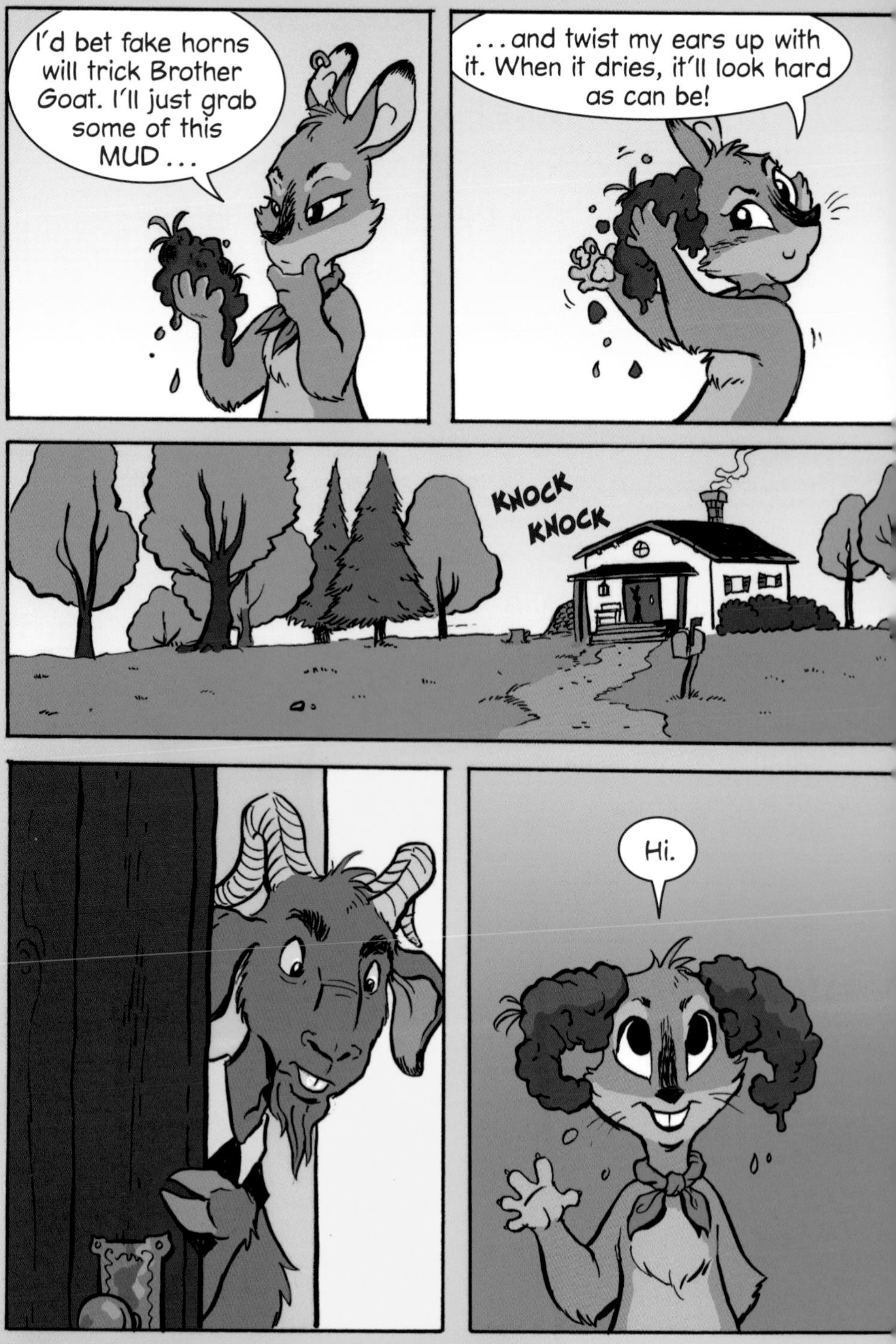

I'd bet fake horns will trick Brother Goat. I'll just grab some of this MUD . . .
. . . and twist my ears up with it. When it dries, it'll look hard as can be!
KNOCK KNOCK
Hi.

"Brother Rabbit!" says Goat.

"I'm here for the party," says Rabbit.

Goat frowns. "Um, well, this party is for horned animals only."

Rabbit points at his ears. "But I have horns!" he says. "I met an old witch in the swamp, and she zapped me with her magic."

"Well, then," hoots Horned Owl, "you get to come to Brother Goat's parties."

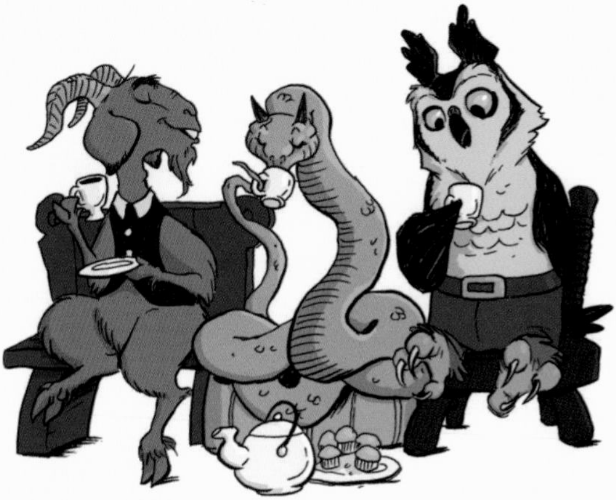

"We like to make listsssss," says Horned Viper.

"I heard about your lists!" says Rabbit, stomping his foot. "Seems you think I'm not clever!"

Go on to the next page.

The animals all look at him in surprise. Rabbit hops up on the table.

If Rabbit demands to be declared the cleverest animal of all,

TURN TO PAGE 61.

If Rabbit proves how clever he is with a trick,

TURN TO PAGE 34.

Rabbit scoops up the turtle. He ties the turtle to a stick and straps the stick to a helmet.

"Ooh, I almost forgot!" he says. He pops the helmet on Fox's head before Fox has a chance to see what Rabbit has done. "We can't have a race without safety! Now...GO!"

Fox takes off running. Little does he know that the turtle will always be just ahead of him.

Rabbit laughs. Fox will lose a race to the slowest animal in the woods. It looks as if Rabbit is the cleverest trickster after all!

THE END

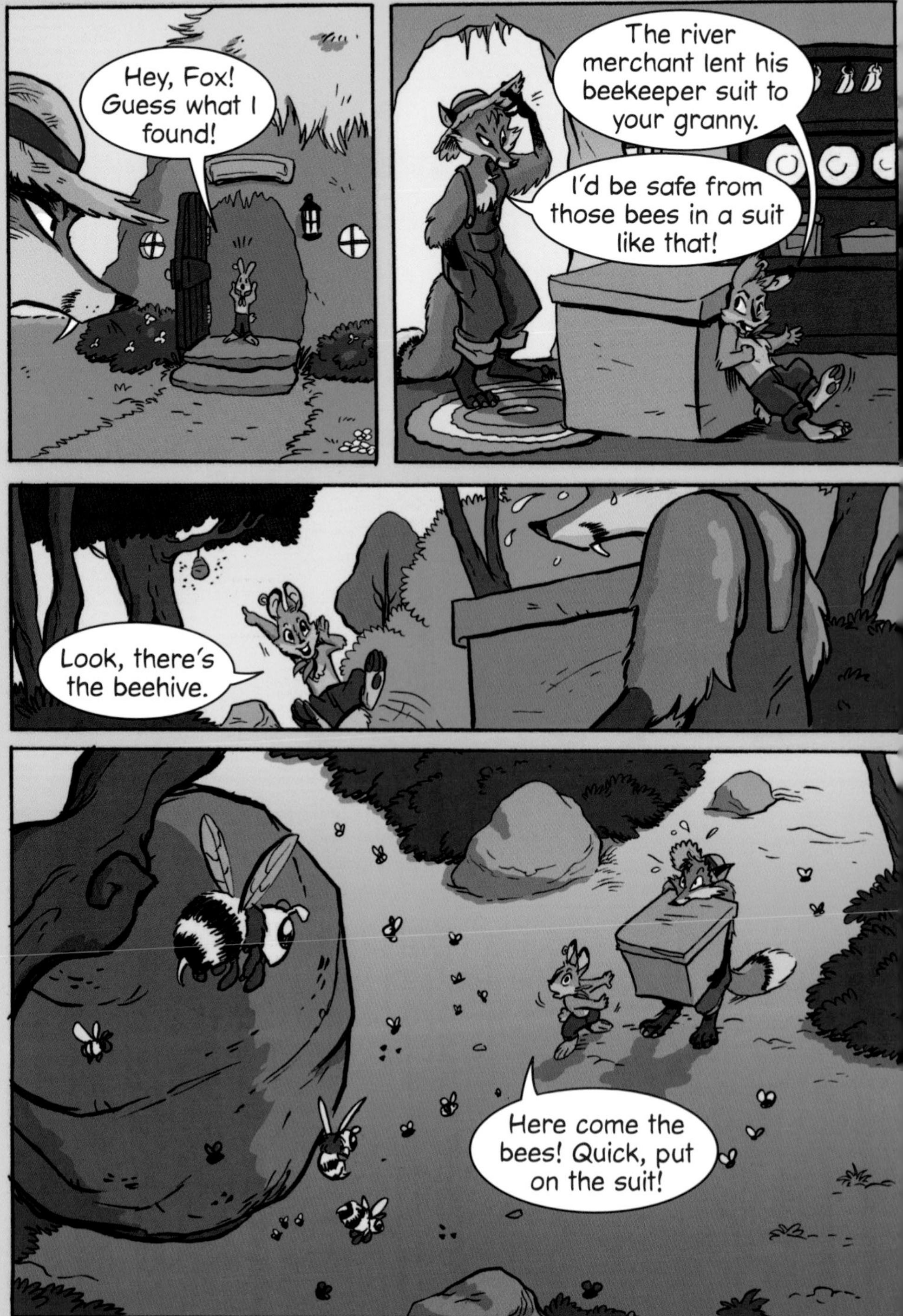
Hey, Fox! Guess what I found!
The river merchant lent his beekeeper suit to your granny.
I'd be safe from those bees in a suit like that!
Look, there's the beehive.
Here come the bees! Quick, put on the suit!

 Go on to the next page.

Fox opens the box, and Granny Fox pops up. "Is my hair done yet?" she asks.

Fox grabs Granny and runs off.

Rabbit keeps laughing—until he feels a sharp sting. "Ouch!" he yells.

He forgot the bees might sting HIM. He runs, too, with a cloud of bees behind him. He'd better keep running, or this will be

THE END

"I've got to get those antlers, alligators or no alligators," says Rabbit.

Rabbit sees a log floating by. He hops on. Pretty soon he's almost to Bear's cave.

"I'm glad I didn't see any gators!" he says.

"That's a terrible thing to say," says the log in a deep, rumbling voice. "Who wouldn't want to see me?"

Rabbit is so startled that he falls into the water. This log is no log at all—it's an alligator!

"Now, I think I'll take you home to my poor, hungry children," says the alligator. "They miss their mother so, but I have to go out every day to find them food!"

"Sister Gator, you don't want to eat me!" exclaims Rabbit.

If Rabbit tells her that he is part alligator,

TURN TO PAGE 40.

If Rabbit offers to be the baby alligators' babysitter,

TURN TO PAGE 25.

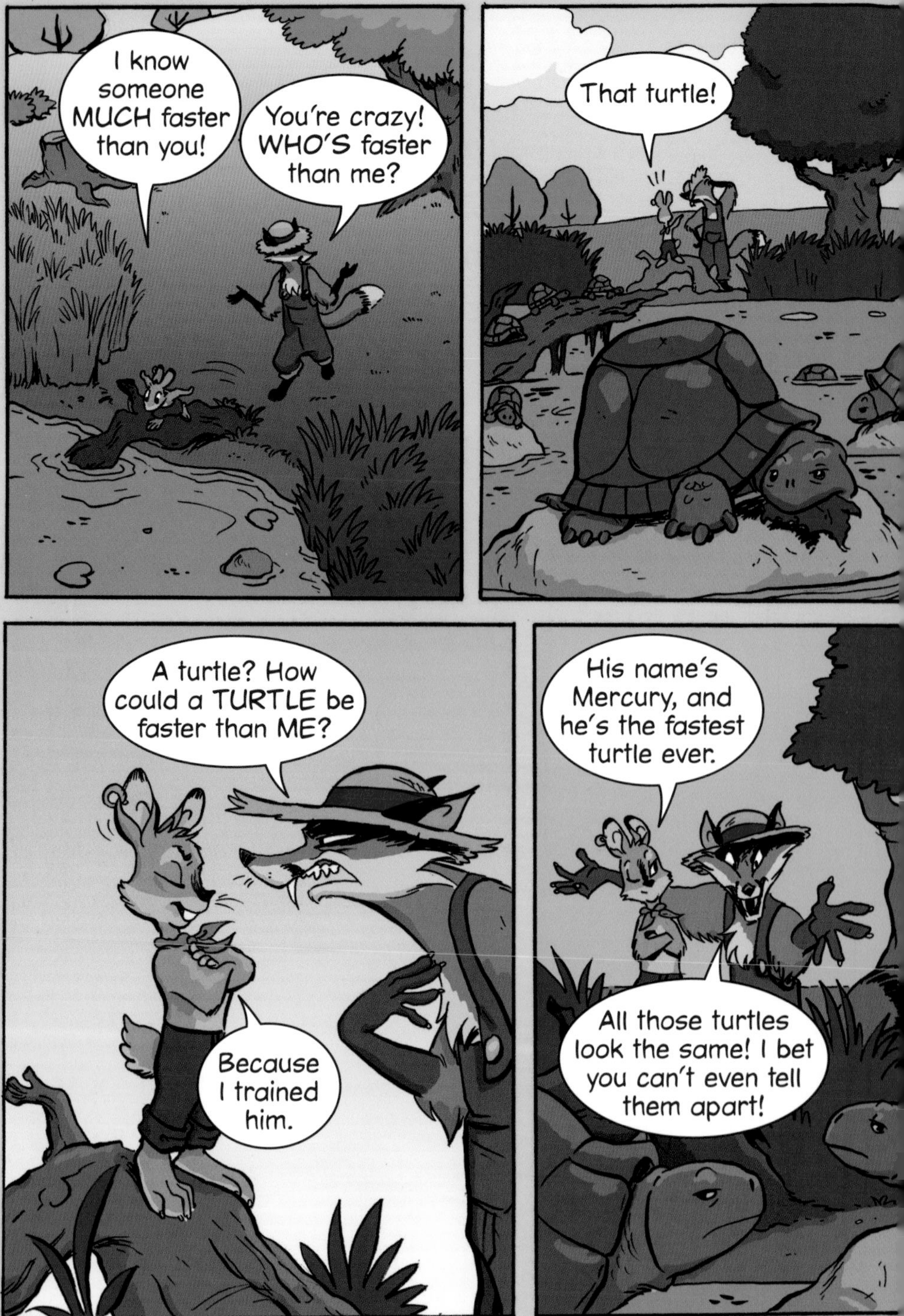
I know someone MUCH faster than you!
You're crazy! WHO'S faster than me?
That turtle!
A turtle? How could a TURTLE be faster than ME?
Because I trained him.
His name's Mercury, and he's the fastest turtle ever.
All those turtles look the same! I bet you can't even tell them apart!

 Go on to the next page.

"You're just scared to race him!" says Rabbit. "But you'd better if you want to keep telling people that you're fast!"

If Rabbit tries to get Fox to race Mercury the turtle,

TURN TO PAGE 59.

If Rabbit tries to trick Fox into refusing to race Mercury,

TURN TO PAGE 13.

23

"You don't want to eat us, Brother Gator,"
says Rabbit. "We're ghosts!"

"I like ghosts! My best friend is a ghost too,"
Gator says. "Look, here he comes now!"

Fox and Rabbit look up to see something
floating toward them.

"I thought you made up the haunted gator
place to trick me," says Fox.

"I thought I did too!" says Rabbit, covering his
eyes. His scary trick has turned out to be too
scary for his own good!

THE END

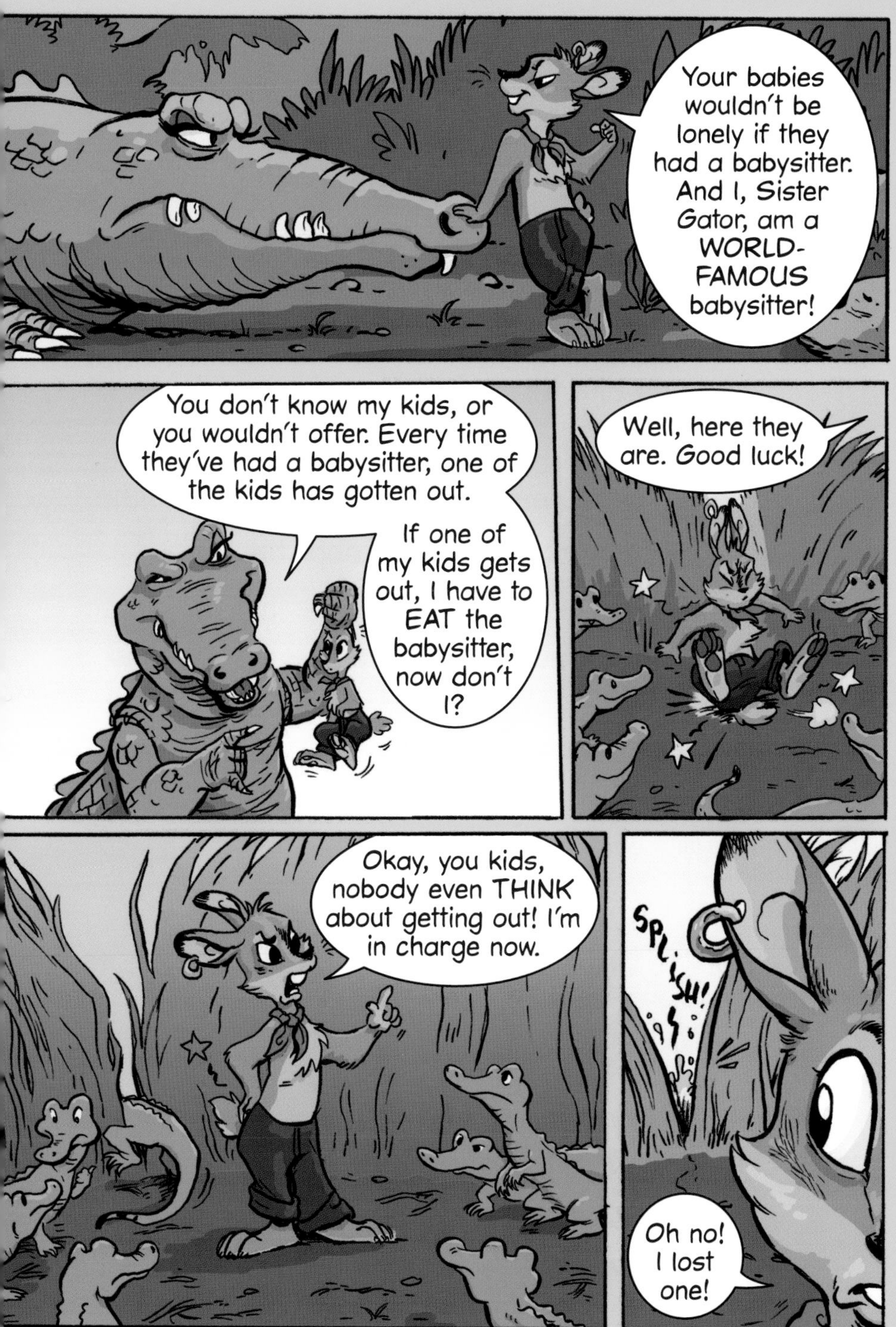
Your babies wouldn't be lonely if they had a babysitter. And I, Sister Gator, am a WORLD-FAMOUS babysitter!
You don't know my kids, or you wouldn't offer. Every time they've had a babysitter, one of the kids has gotten out.
If one of my kids gets out, I have to EAT the babysitter, now don't I?
Well, here they are. Good luck!
Okay, you kids, nobody even THINK about getting out! I'm in charge now.
SPLISH!
Oh no! I lost one!

"Time for the babies' baths," says Sister Gator when she returns. "Hand them to me one at a time."

When it's time to pass her number seven, Rabbit has an idea! He grabs one of the clean kids, drags him through the mud, and hands him to Gator.

"Seven," she counts. "You did well today, little bunny! I won't eat you if you keep this up."

Rabbit watches two babies slide into the water. Looks as if he'll need lots of tricks to survive his new job!

THE END

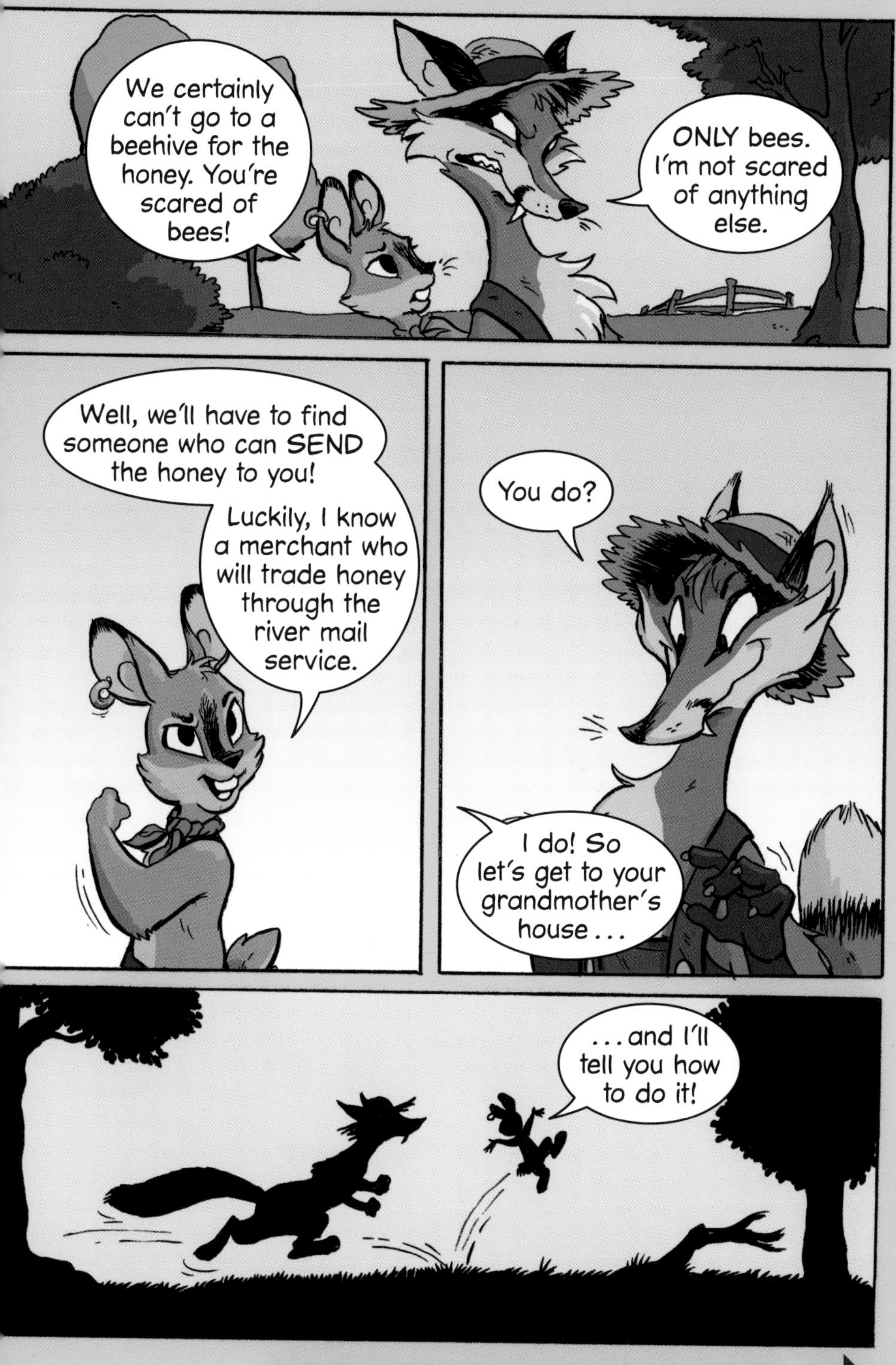
We certainly can't go to a beehive for the honey. You're scared of bees!
ONLY bees. I'm not scared of anything else.
Well, we'll have to find someone who can SEND the honey to you!
Luckily, I know a merchant who will trade honey through the river mail service.
You do?
I do! So let's get to your grandmother's house . . .
. . . and I'll tell you how to do it!

Rabbit and Fox run to Granny Fox's house. "Better let me go in first," says Rabbit. He ducks into the house, grinning. The best way to trick Fox is to trick his grandmother first!

"Brother Rabbit, is that you?" exclaims Granny Fox. "What are you doing here?"

If Rabbit tricks Granny Fox into hiding in a box,

TURN TO PAGE 42.

If Rabbit tricks Granny Fox into scaring Fox,

TURN TO PAGE 56.

"I'll take you," says Rabbit, hopping away. Fox runs behind him.

Rabbit hops deeper and deeper into the woods. It gets darker with each passing minute. He's sure that Fox won't be able to find his way out.

"We're lost!" he says to Fox. "Are you scared yet, Brother Fox?"

"Who, me?" asks Fox. "No. But seeing as we're lost and I'm hungry..."

Fox grabs Rabbit by the ears. Rabbit looks at Fox's big teeth and realizes that this trick has brought him to

THE END

"Well," says Rabbit, shrugging his shoulders, "I may not be the cleverest animal. I suppose that's true."

Fox glares at him. "Say," he growls. "I've never known YOU to be humble. Is this a trick?"

Rabbit shakes his head. "No trick," he says. "I don't have to be clever. There are lots of things that I'm proud of about myself."

"Like what?" asks Fox.

"Oh, I don't want to toot my own horn," says Rabbit. "I'd much rather hear what you are best at!"

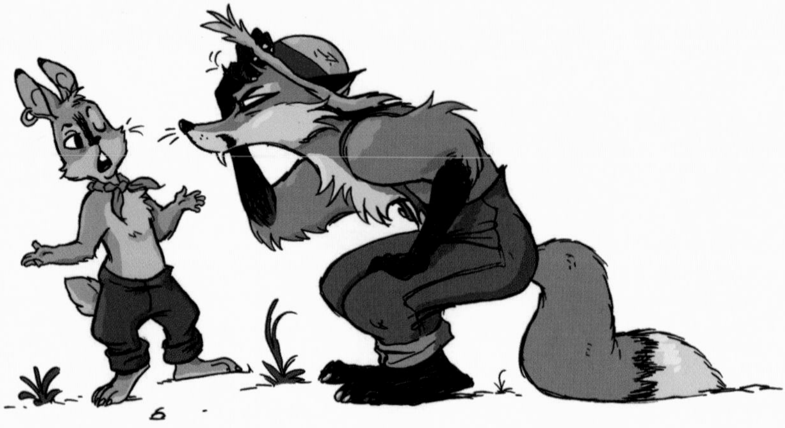

 Go on to the next page.

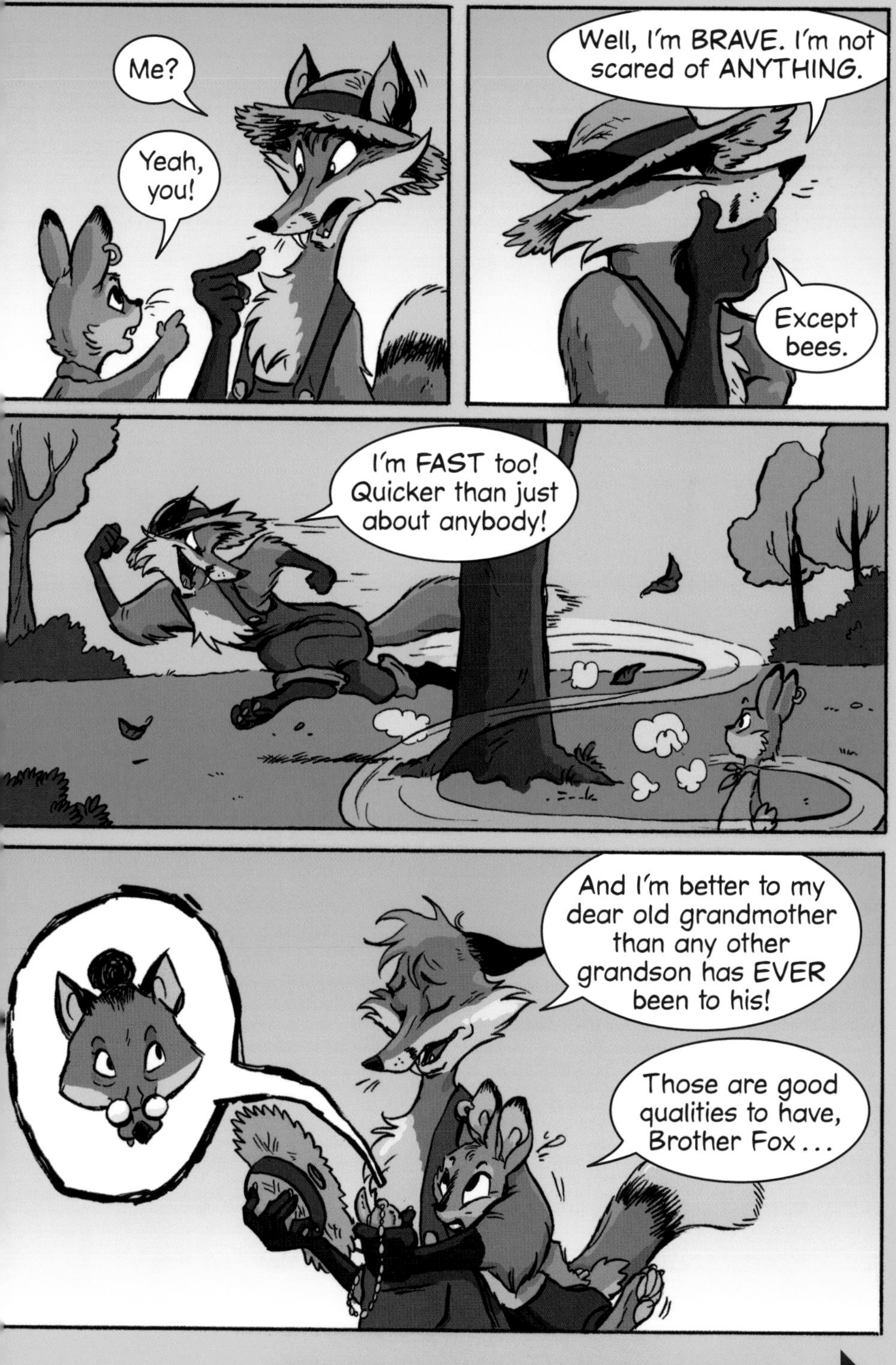
Me?
Yeah, you!
Well, I'm BRAVE. I'm not scared of ANYTHING.
Except bees.
I'm FAST too! Quicker than just about anybody!
And I'm better to my dear old grandmother than any other grandson has EVER been to his!
Those are good qualities to have, Brother Fox . . .

Go on to the next page.

"...but I'm afraid I have you beat when it comes to one of them!"

Rabbit has a trick up his sleeve. He's going to use Fox's pride against him!

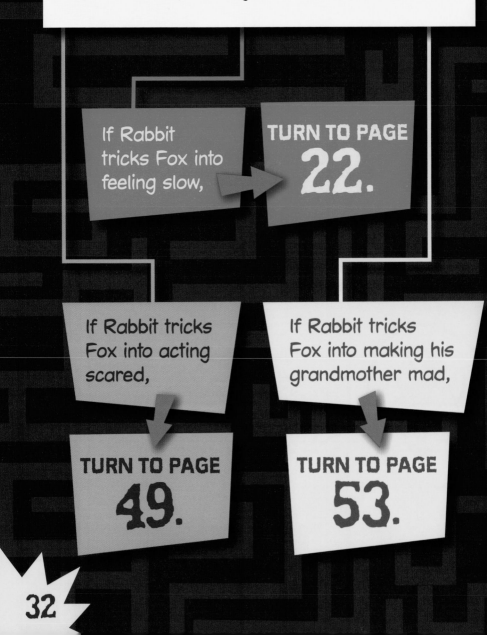

If Rabbit tricks Fox into feeling slow,
TURN TO PAGE 22.

If Rabbit tricks Fox into acting scared,
TURN TO PAGE 49.

If Rabbit tricks Fox into making his grandmother mad,
TURN TO PAGE 53.

"I want you to give me all your snacks!" booms Rabbit.

"All right," whimpers Bear. "Follow me."

Rabbit follows Bear into the cave. Rabbit sees a huge treasure of candy, popcorn, and every treat he can imagine! As he reaches for them, Bear grabs his arm.

"I couldn't see in the bright sunlight," says Bear, "but I can see in here. You're no tree monster—you just want my snacks! Well, now you are the snack!" He licks his lips, and Rabbit knows that this is

THE END

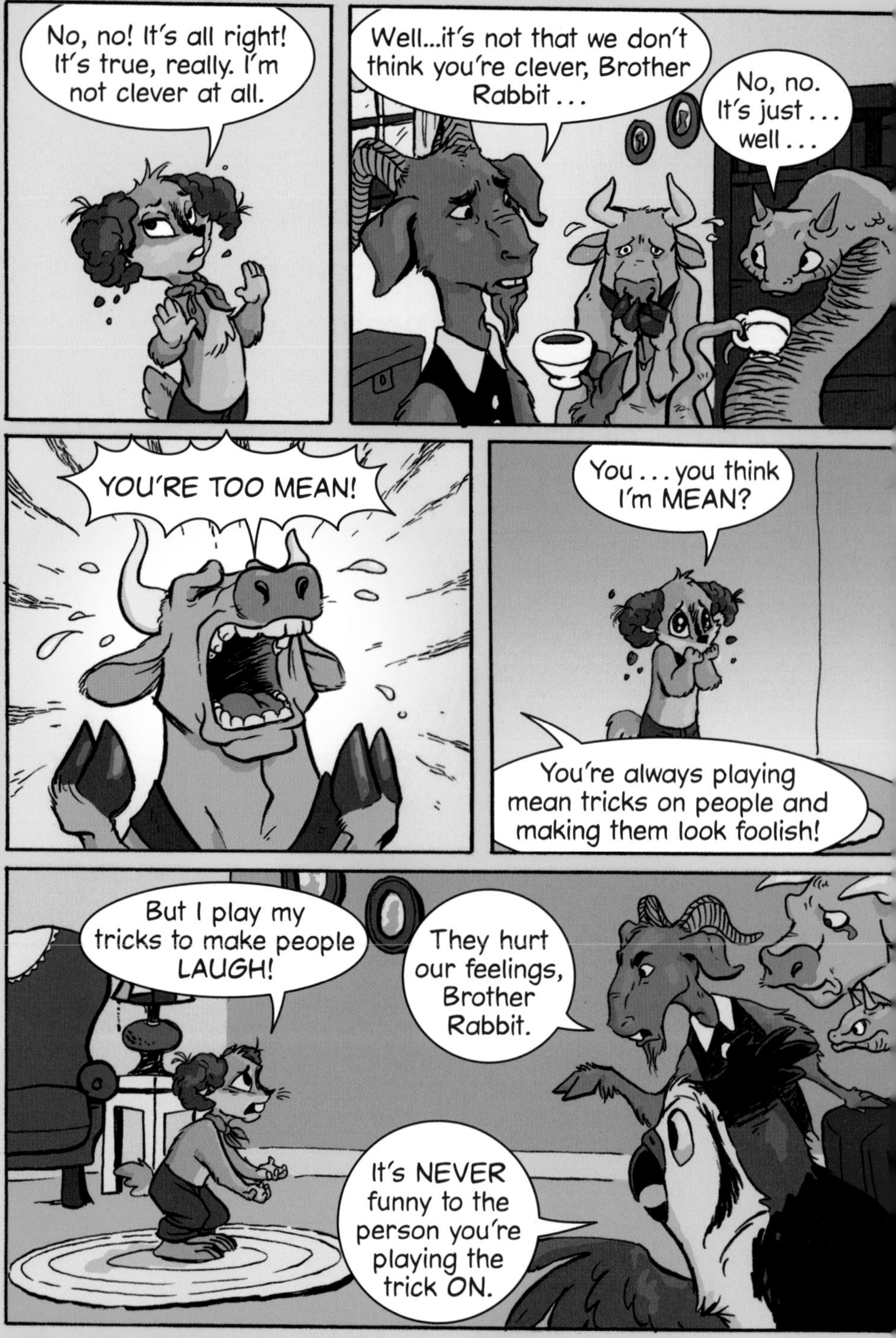
No, no! It's all right! It's true, really. I'm not clever at all.
Well...it's not that we don't think you're clever, Brother Rabbit . . .
No, no. It's just . . . well . . .
YOU'RE TOO MEAN!
You . . . you think I'm MEAN?
You're always playing mean tricks on people and making them look foolish!
But I play my tricks to make people LAUGH!
They hurt our feelings, Brother Rabbit.
It's NEVER funny to the person you're playing the trick ON.

"I didn't know my tricks made people sad," says Rabbit. He shuffles sadly toward the door. "I'm sorry!"

"Rabbit," says Goat, "you're sorry you hurt our feelings. That means you're smart enough to learn from your mistakes. You're the cleverest animal on my list!"

"Mine, too!" say the others. They invite him to eat and tell him some nicer ways to make his friends laugh.

"Well, I do know some pretty good jokes," Rabbit says, smiling. "Knock, knock..."

THE END

"Let's go to your grandmother's house," says Rabbit. "You can show me how good a grandson you really are!"

As they set out, Rabbit's mind is working hard. What trick can he pull? He starts to have an idea . . . but then he's picked up by the ears and stuffed into an old bag.

"My grandmother loves rabbit stew!" says Fox, licking his lips. "So you see, I am a wonderful grandson."

Looks as if Rabbit isn't so clever after all! For him, this is

THE END

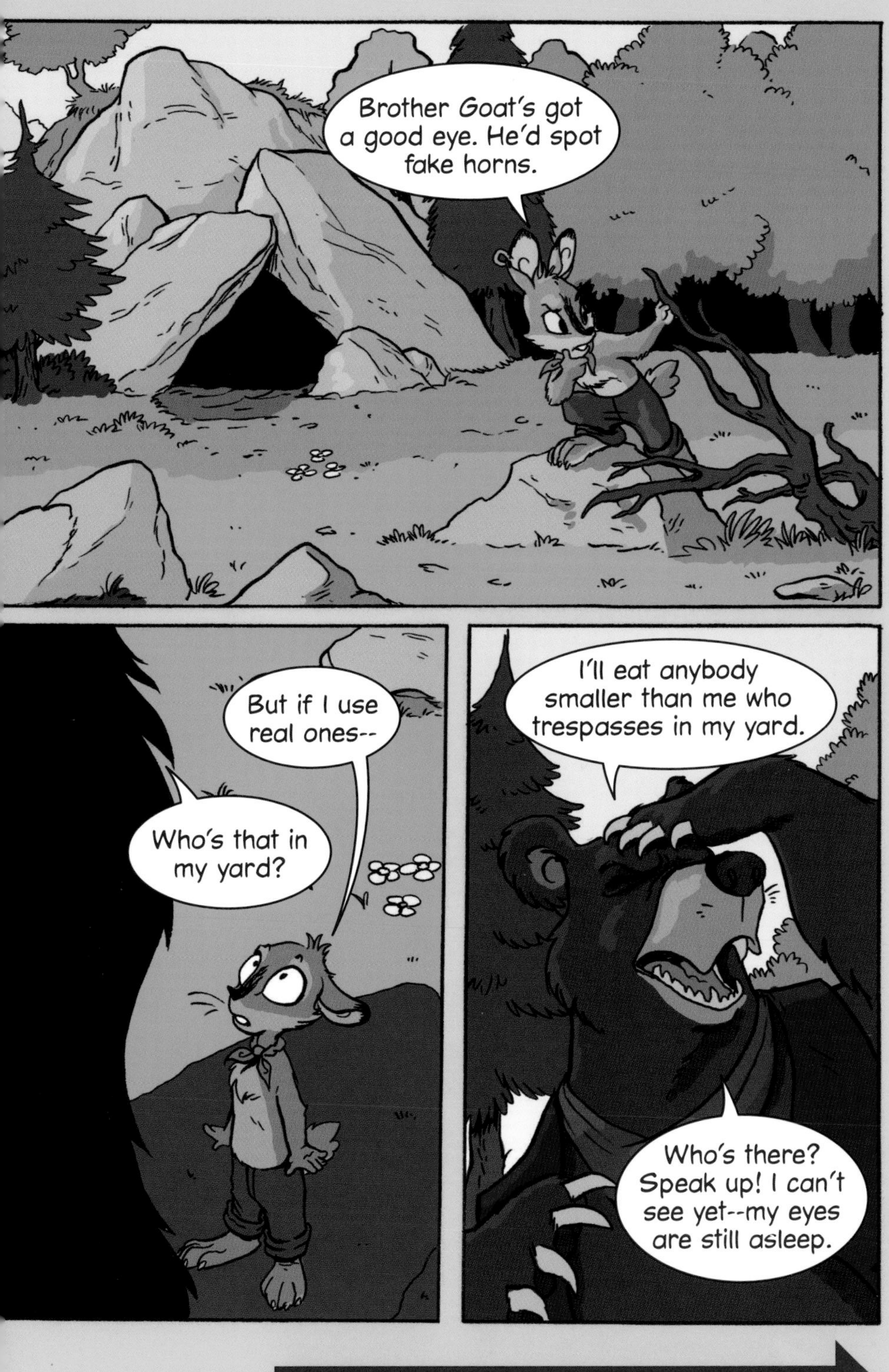
Brother Goat's got a good eye. He'd spot fake horns.
But if I use real ones--
Who's that in my yard?
I'll eat anybody smaller than me who trespasses in my yard.
Who's there? Speak up! I can't see yet--my eyes are still asleep.

Go on to the next page.

Rabbit better think fast! Bear seems mad...
AND hungry.

If Rabbit tries to
be very quiet,

TURN TO PAGE
58.

If Rabbit pretends to
be bigger than Bear,

TURN TO PAGE
11.

"I put a ham in this box," says Rabbit. "We'll mail it down the river to the honey merchants, and they'll send you some honey in return."

"Sounds good," Fox says. He carries the box to the river and tosses it in.

Granny Fox bursts through the top. "Fool grandson!" she yells. "Why did you throw me in the river? My hair isn't done yet!"

"Hold on, Granny, I'm coming!" shouts Fox, jumping in the river. Rabbit laughs and laughs as he sees them float out of sight.

THE END

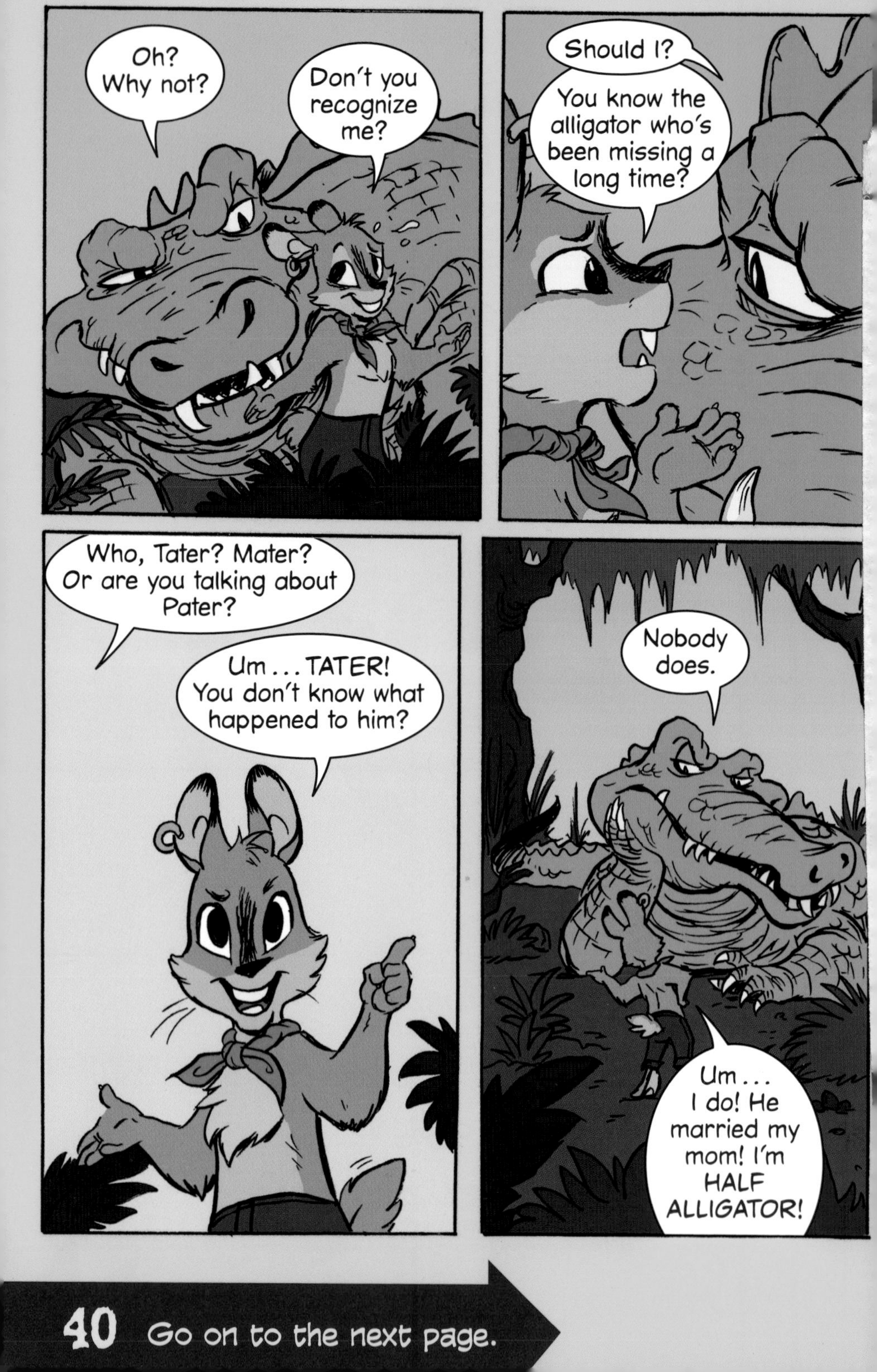
Oh? Why not?
Don't you recognize me?
Should I?
You know the alligator who's been missing a long time?
Who, Tater? Mater? Or are you talking about Pater?
Um . . . TATER! You don't know what happened to him?
Nobody does.
Um . . . I do! He married my mom! I'm HALF ALLIGATOR!

"Well, I do declare!" yells the alligator, scooping Rabbit up and giving him a big hug. "I never thought I'd see a gator that looks like a bunny! Come with me, little one."

"Actually," starts Rabbit, "I really should be getting home."

"Oh, honey, you ARE home!" says Gator. "You're going to live in the swamp, now!"

Rabbit watches the dry land as it gets farther and farther away. He won't be making it to Goat's lunch...or anywhere else but the soggy, humid swamp!

THE END

"I had to tell you my news!" Rabbit says. "Lately, my hair has been sticking out every which way!"

Granny Fox rubs the top of her head. "Oh, I know how that can be!" she says. "But your hair looks fine!"

"That's because of the box treatment," Rabbit grins. "I got in a box and sat for an hour. It made my hair behave!"

"I have a box!" cries Granny. "Do you think the treatment will work for me?"

"Sure!" says Rabbit. "Get in it. But you have to keep still!"

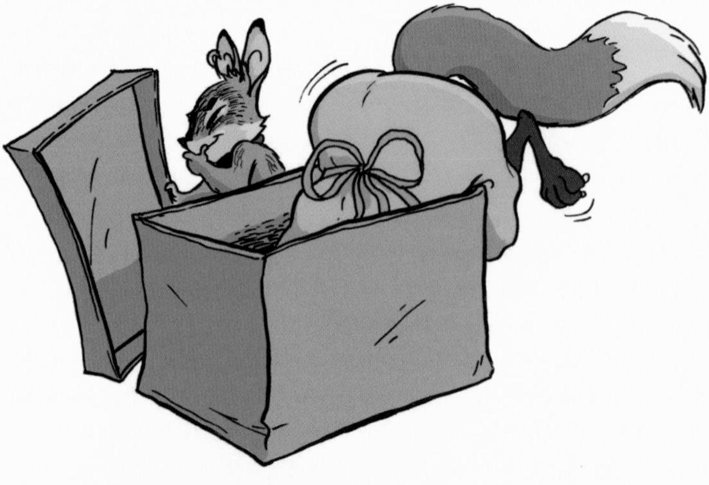

Go on to the next page.

Granny Fox is shut up in the box. Rabbit runs to the door and calls out. "Brother Fox! Your grandmother isn't here, but I know how we can get honey!"

If Rabbit tricks Fox into taking the box to a beehive,

TURN TO PAGE 18.

If Rabbit tricks Fox into sending his grandmother through the mail,

TURN TO PAGE 39.

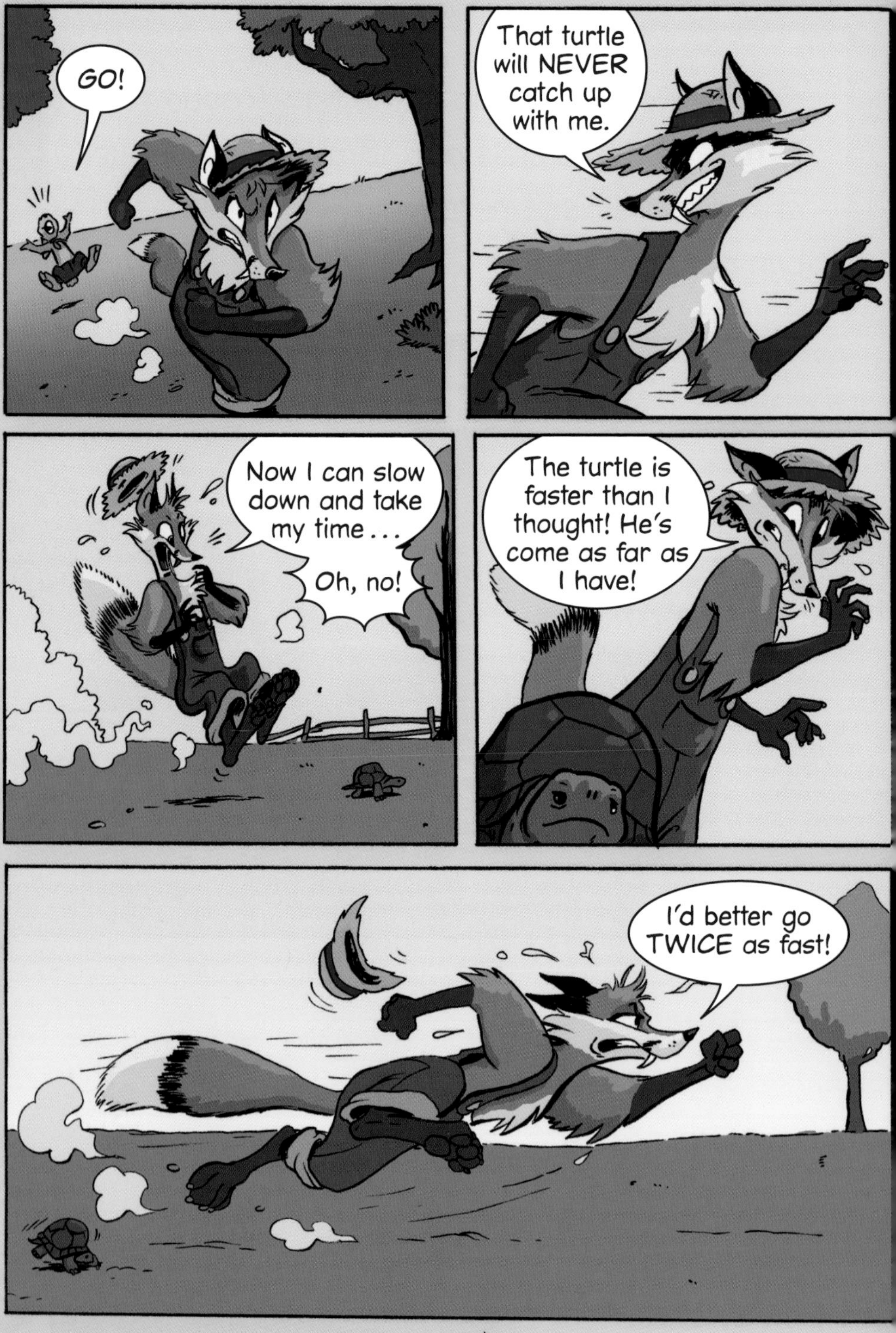
GO!
That turtle will NEVER catch up with me.
Now I can slow down and take my time . . .
Oh, no!
The turtle is faster than I thought! He's come as far as I have!
I'd better go TWICE as fast!

 Go on to the next page.

Fox runs and runs. But every time he looks up, he sees the turtle ahead of him! Pretty soon he plops down, out of breath.

Rabbit arrives, carrying a bag. "Brother Rabbit," Fox wheezes, "how can your turtle run so fast?"

"He can't," answers Rabbit, laughing. "I put a turtle along the road every half mile. So you always thought he was ahead of you!"

"I take back what I said before," gasps Fox, sitting up. "You're the cleverest trickster I've ever met!"

THE END

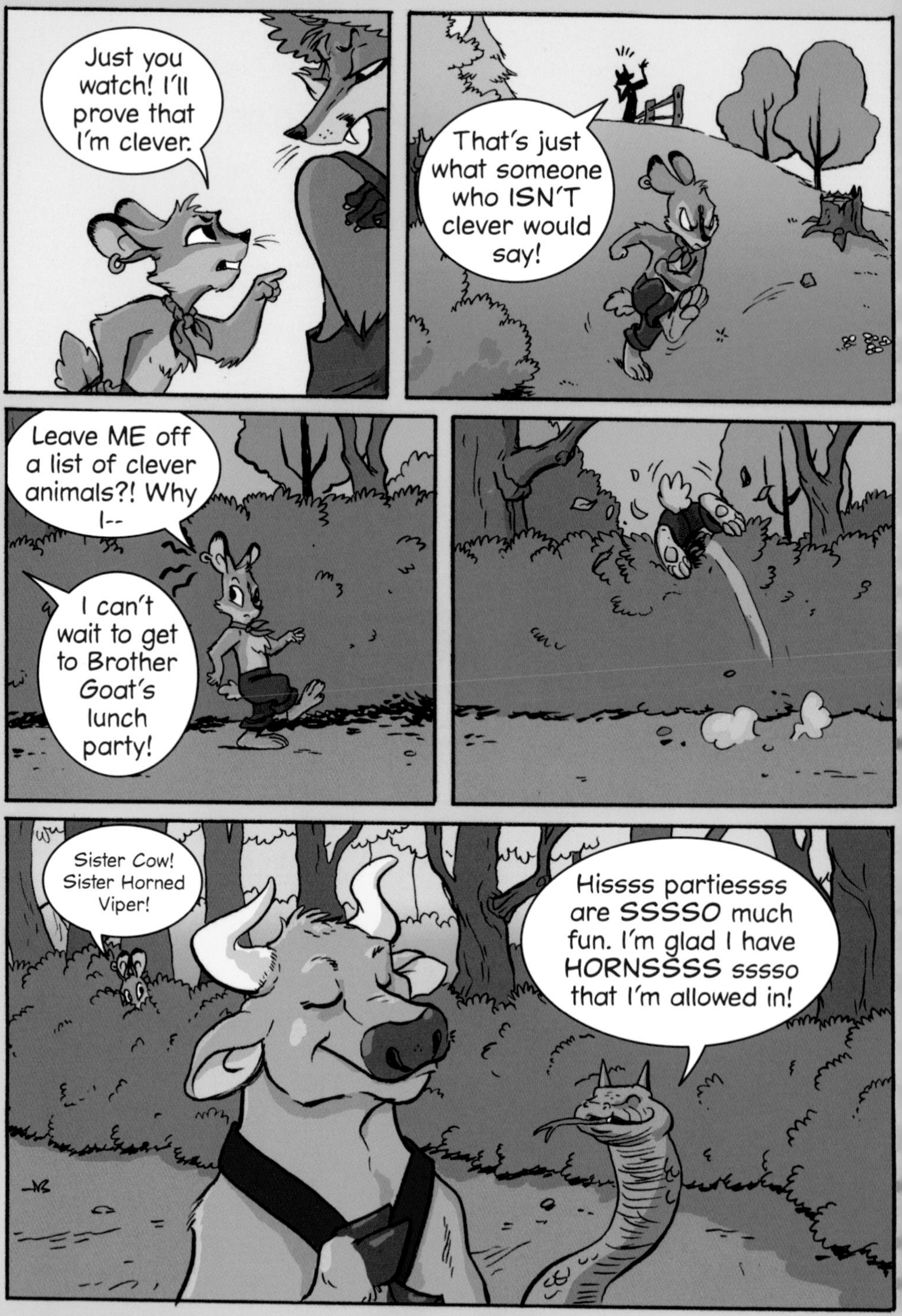
Just you watch! I'll prove that I'm clever.
That's just what someone who ISN'T clever would say!
Leave ME off a list of clever animals?! Why I--
I can't wait to get to Brother Goat's lunch party!
Sister Cow! Sister Horned Viper!
Hissss partiessss are SSSSO much fun. I'm glad I have HORNSSSS sssso that I'm allowed in!

"Horns!" says Rabbit to himself. "I'd better get some if I want to go to this party."

Rabbit runs deeper into the woods. He calls for his friend, "Brother Buck!"

"Brother Rabbit!" comes a low reply.

"Brother Buck, what happened to your fine antlers?" asks Rabbit. "They were so big!"

Buck laughs. "My antlers fall off every year. I grow new ones."

Rabbit's eyes get wide. "Could I have your old ones?"

"Why not?" Buck shrugs. "I left them by Brother Bear's cave, near the swamp."

Go on to the next page.

"Thanks, Brother Buck!" says Rabbit, as he hops off. "I need antlers if I want to go to Brother Goat's party. But the swamp is full of alligators. And Brother Bear gets furious if anyone cuts through his yard. Maybe I should make some horns myself."

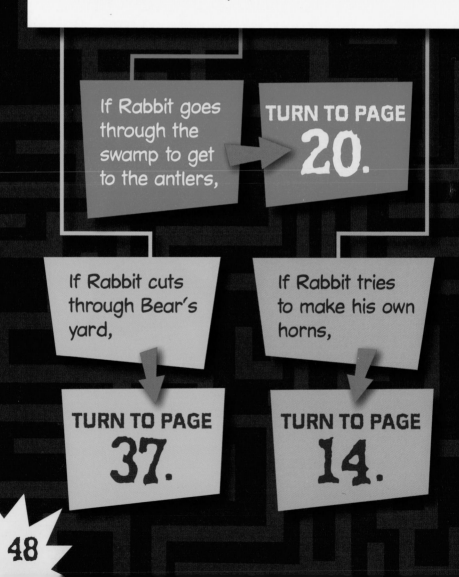

If Rabbit goes through the swamp to get to the antlers,

TURN TO PAGE 20.

If Rabbit cuts through Bear's yard,

TURN TO PAGE 37.

If Rabbit tries to make his own horns,

TURN TO PAGE 14.

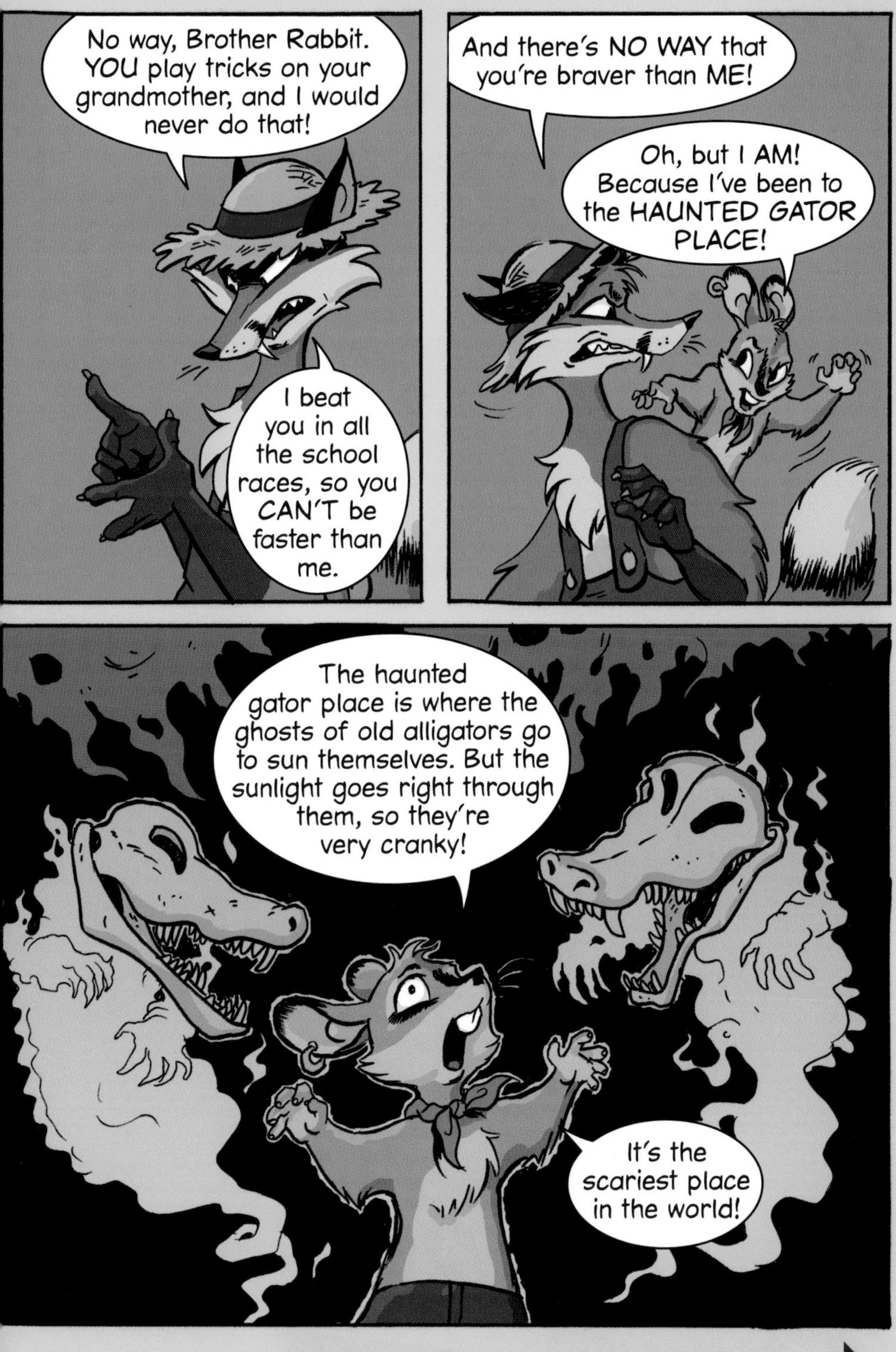
No way, Brother Rabbit. YOU play tricks on your grandmother, and I would never do that!
I beat you in all the school races, so you CAN'T be faster than me.
And there's NO WAY that you're braver than ME!
Oh, but I AM! Because I've been to the HAUNTED GATOR PLACE!
The haunted gator place is where the ghosts of old alligators go to sun themselves. But the sunlight goes right through them, so they're very cranky!
It's the scariest place in the world!

Go on to the next page.

"Pssshh!" hisses Fox. "That doesn't scare me. Remember, I'm brave! Take me to the haunted gator place. I'll prove I'm braver than you!"

If Rabbit takes Fox to where the real alligators sleep,

TURN TO PAGE 7.

If Rabbit tries to make Fox get lost in the spooky part of the woods,

TURN TO PAGE 29.

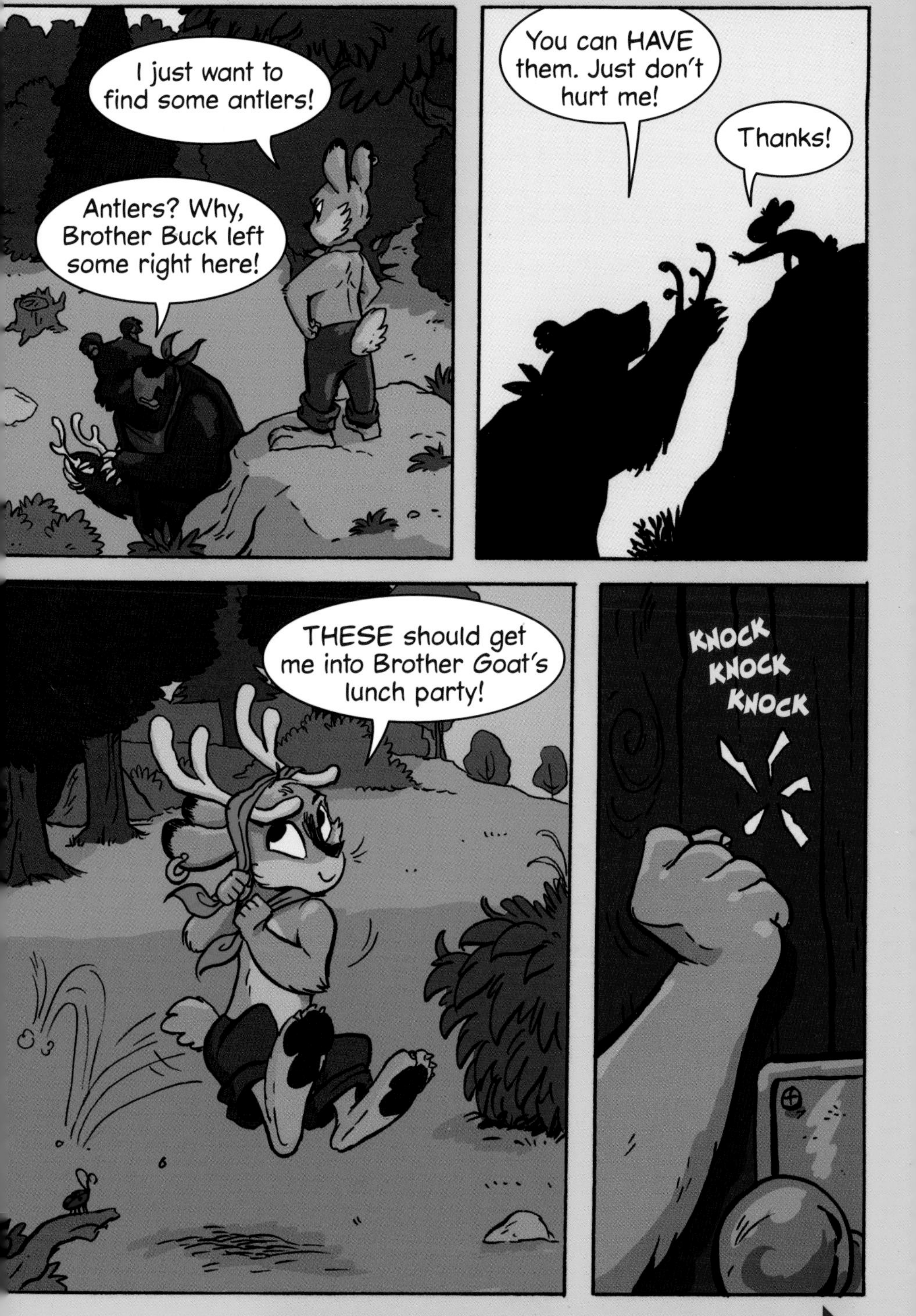
I just want to find some antlers!
Antlers? Why, Brother Buck left some right here!
You can HAVE them. Just don't hurt me!
Thanks!
THESE should get me into Brother Goat's lunch party!
KNOCK
KNOCK
KNOCK

Go on to the next page.

"Hello," says Rabbit, as Goat opens the door. "My name is Jackelope. I heard there's a party for horned animals today."

"Come on in," says Goat. "You look like Brother Rabbit. We were just talking about how clever he is!"

"I thought you told Fox that Rabbit isn't clever at all!" exclaims Rabbit.

"Fox is just jealous that he wasn't on the list," says Goat. "Rabbit is the cleverest animal in the woods."

Rabbit smiles. This is going to be the best party all year.

THE END

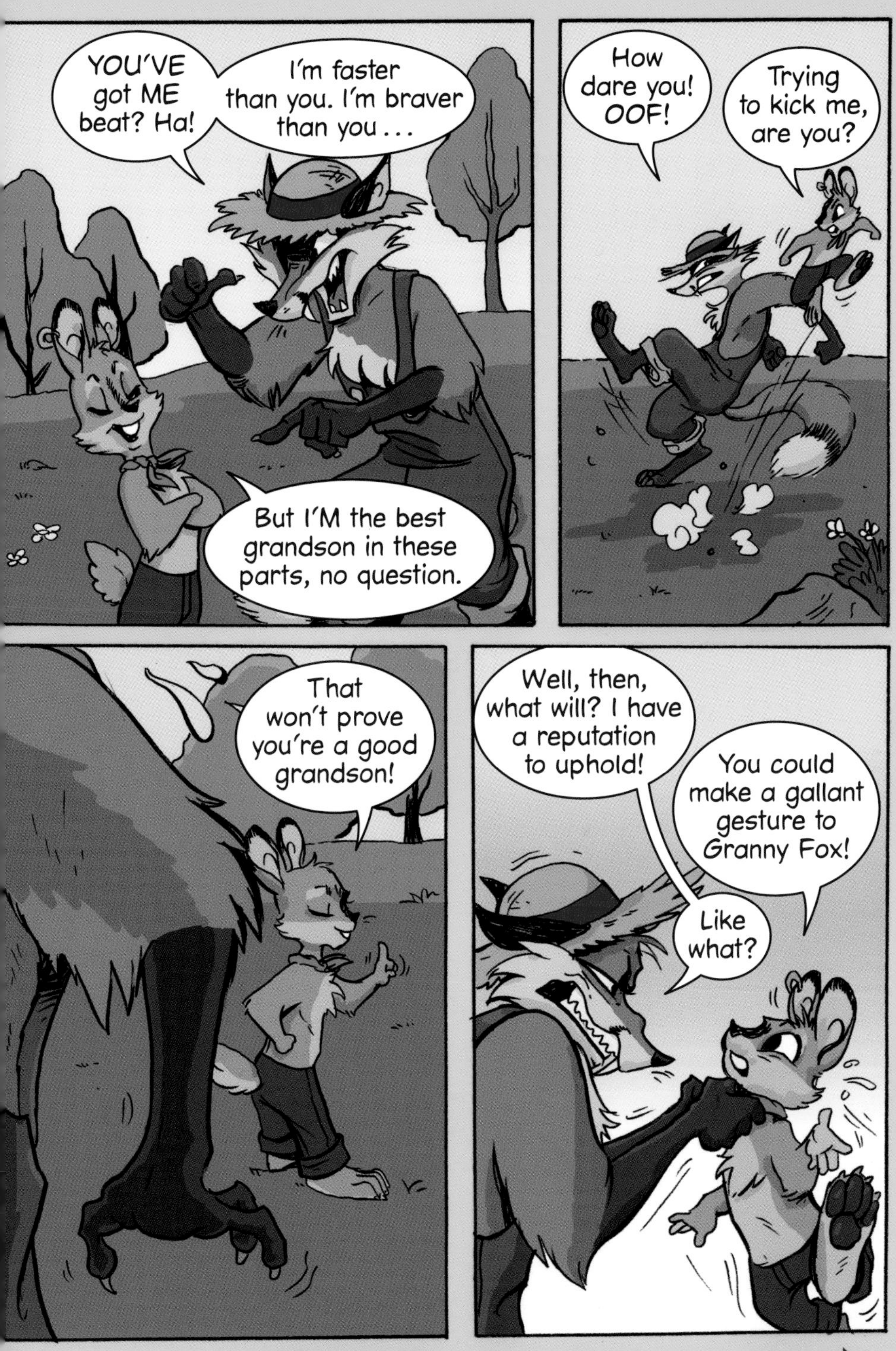
YOU'VE got ME beat? Ha!
I'm faster than you. I'm braver than you . . .
But I'M the best grandson in these parts, no question.
How dare you! OOF!
Trying to kick me, are you?
That won't prove you're a good grandson!
Well, then, what will? I have a reputation to uphold!
You could make a gallant gesture to Granny Fox!
Like what?

Go on to the next page.

Rabbit is ready to spring his trick! But what should he do next? Fox is scared of bees. Maybe Rabbit could trick him into meeting some. Or perhaps Rabbit should go to Granny Fox's house and see if he gets any ideas there.

If Rabbit tricks Fox into meeting some bees,

TURN TO PAGE **9.**

If Rabbit asks to go to Granny Fox's house,

TURN TO PAGE **36.**

"Oh, please, Brother Gator," cries Rabbit, "don't eat me! I'm too young!"

Fox starts to laugh. So does the alligator. Pretty soon they're laughing so hard that they can barely stand.

"Say," Rabbit growls. "What's going on?"

Fox wipes a tear away. "Brother Gator and I are best friends! We were just playing."

"Oh, Rabbit, you were so easy to trick," howls Gator.

Rabbit scowls. He knows that Fox won't let him forget this trick!

THE END

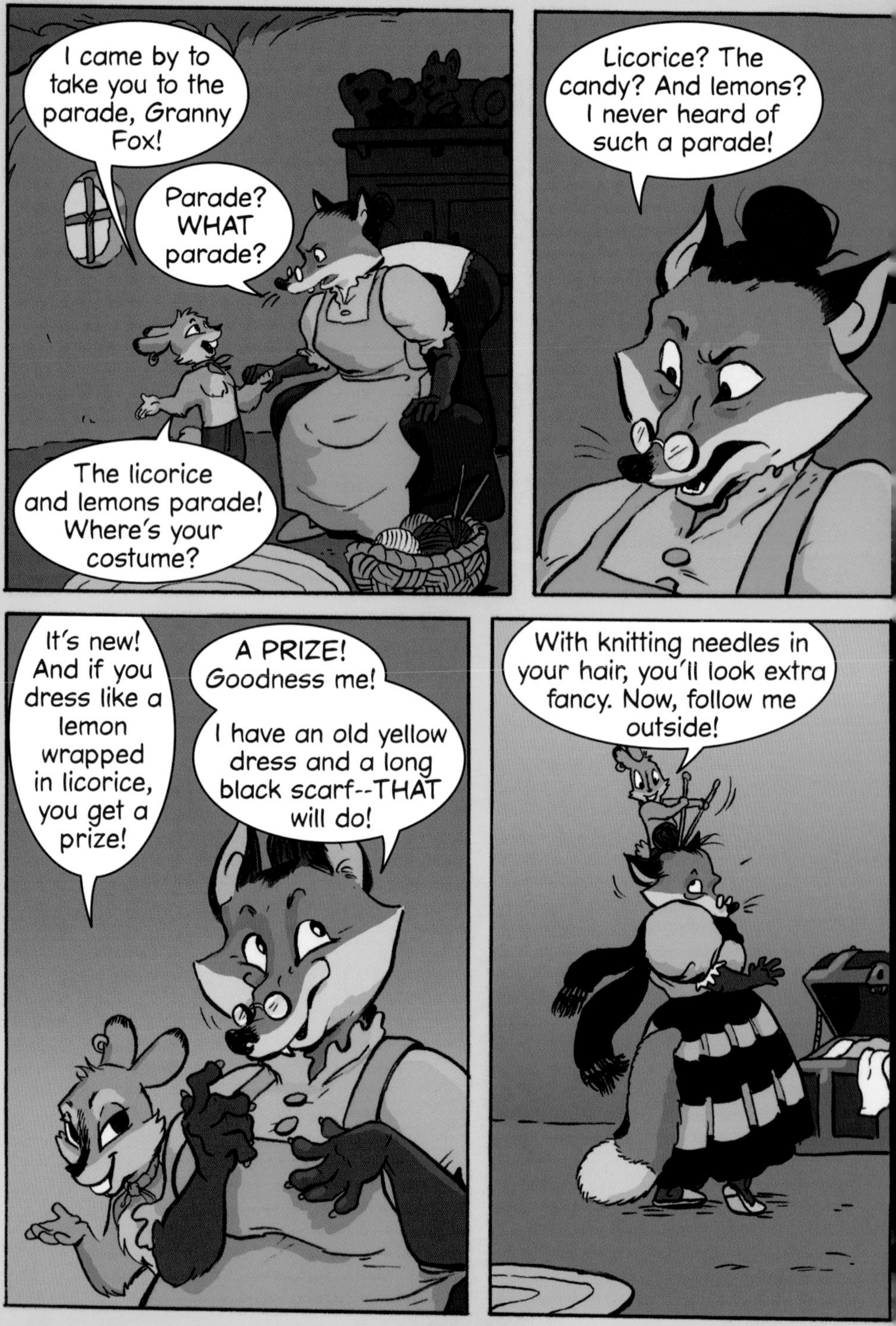
I came by to take you to the parade, Granny Fox!
Parade? WHAT parade?
The licorice and lemons parade! Where's your costume?
Licorice? The candy? And lemons? I never heard of such a parade!
It's new! And if you dress like a lemon wrapped in licorice, you get a prize!
A PRIZE! Goodness me!
I have an old yellow dress and a long black scarf--THAT will do!
With knitting needles in your hair, you'll look extra fancy. Now, follow me outside!

 Go on to the next page.

With that, Rabbit runs out the front door.

"Run!" he yells to Brother Fox. "Your grandmother has turned into a giant bee!"

"That's ridiculous," says Fox. "That can't..."

"Hello, Grandson!" calls Granny Fox, in her yellow dress and black scarf.

"AAAAAAAH!" screams Fox, running off into the woods.

Granny Fox looks over at Rabbit. "Well!" she says. "What a foolish grandson! Rabbit, how about we skip the parade, and I'll make you a wonderful stew?"

"Yes, ma'am!" says Rabbit, hopping inside, smiling.

THE END

Rabbit holds his breath and stands very still. Bear starts to sniff.

Soon, Bear's nose is inches from Rabbit's face. Rabbit is starting to turn blue. He just can't hold his breath anymore. He takes a big breath. Bear hears it and grabs him!

"I told you kids to stay out of my yard!" growls Bear as he takes Rabbit back into his cave. "Oh, well. At least I get a snack before I go back to sleep."

Rabbit gulps. Looks like this is

THE END

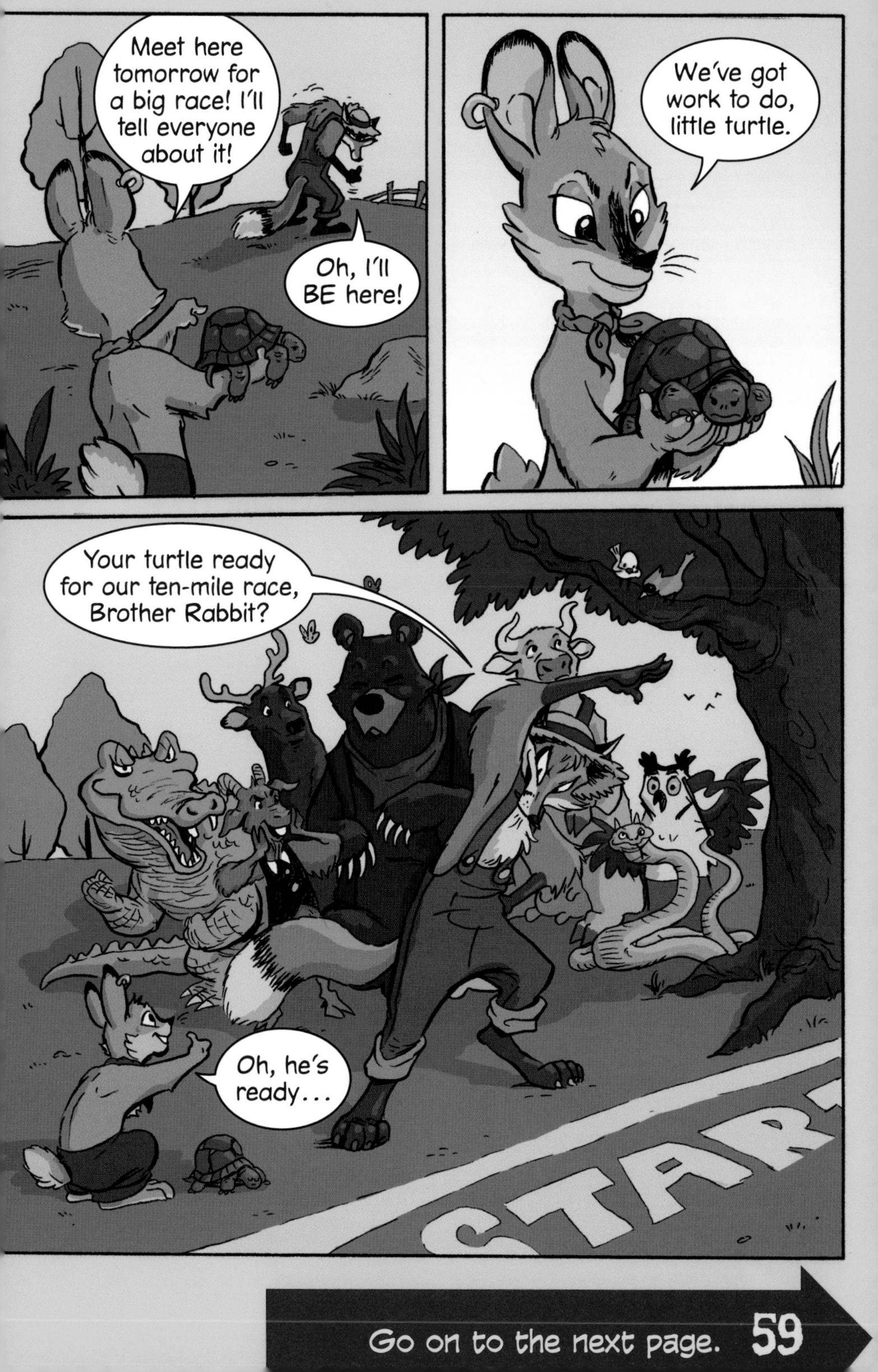
Meet here tomorrow for a big race! I'll tell everyone about it!
Oh, I'll BE here!
We've got work to do, little turtle.
Your turtle ready for our ten-mile race, Brother Rabbit?
Oh, he's ready...
START

"...on your mark, get set..."

Rabbit spent all night planning. Now it's time to see his plan in action!

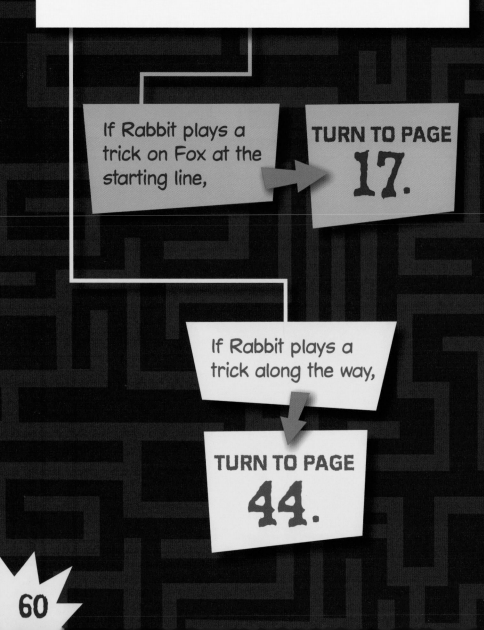

If Rabbit plays a trick on Fox at the starting line,

TURN TO PAGE 17.

If Rabbit plays a trick along the way,

TURN TO PAGE 44.

"Put me on the list of the cleverest animals!" shouts Rabbit, jumping up and down.

"You foolish rabbit!" shouts Goat. "We never made a list of the CLEVEREST animals. We made a list of the HEAVIEST animals!"

Rabbit stops jumping. "But Brother Fox said—"

Goat cuts him off. "Fox must have misheard us. But that's no excuse for you to throw a tantrum!"

Goat and the others toss Rabbit out into the mud. Maybe next time he won't be so rude!

THE END

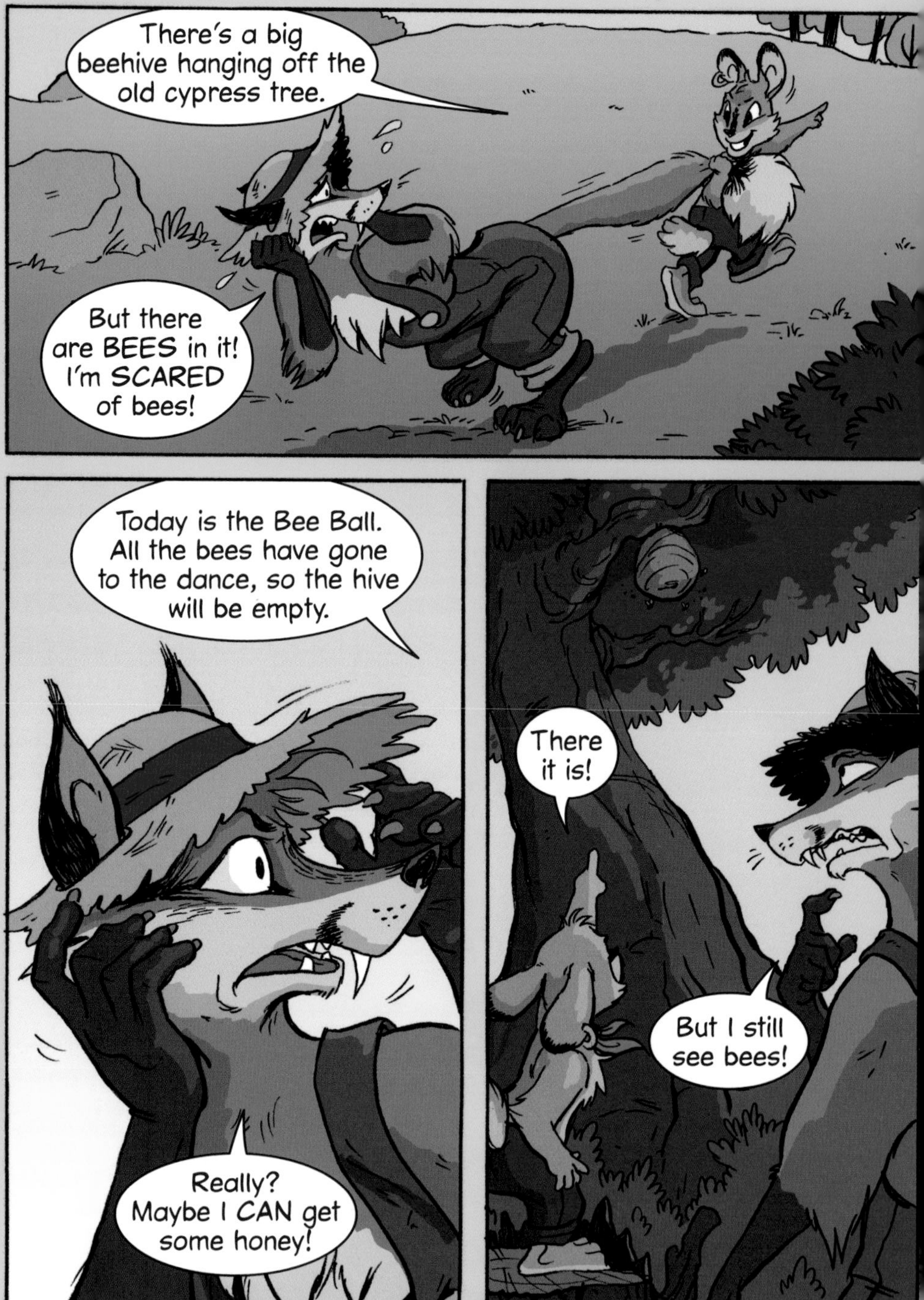
There's a big beehive hanging off the old cypress tree.
But there are BEES in it! I'm SCARED of bees!
Today is the Bee Ball. All the bees have gone to the dance, so the hive will be empty.
Really? Maybe I CAN get some honey!
There it is!
But I still see bees!

Go on to the next page.

Rabbit shimmies up the tree and looks into the hive. It is FULL of bees!

"Only two bees left, and they're just leaving," calls Rabbit. "I'll knock the nest down for you."

Fox catches the hive. "Got it!" he calls. "Mmmm, honey."

Suddenly, a whole swarm of angry bees fly out! Fox drops the hive and runs.

"You may not think I'm clever, Brother Fox, but I tricked you into holding an armload of bees!" laughs Rabbit.

THE END

The **RABBIT** stories come from the southeastern United States. Many of them developed from old stories told in the 1800s. People were taken from Africa and forced to work as slaves on southern plantations. They brought their stories with them.

Over time, the African stories changed to reflect life in America. Storytellers began using local animals such as bears and alligators, rather than African animals such as lions and elephants.

Two types of Rabbit stories were most common. In one, Rabbit tricks other animals, usually animals bigger than himself. People liked to tell stories in which Rabbit tricked animals into letting him go, because they wanted to be set free themselves.

The other type of story was used to teach children manners. If animals were rude or cruel, didn't pay attention in church or school, or didn't say please and thank you, bad things would happen to them. Rabbit got in trouble more than once because he behaved badly!

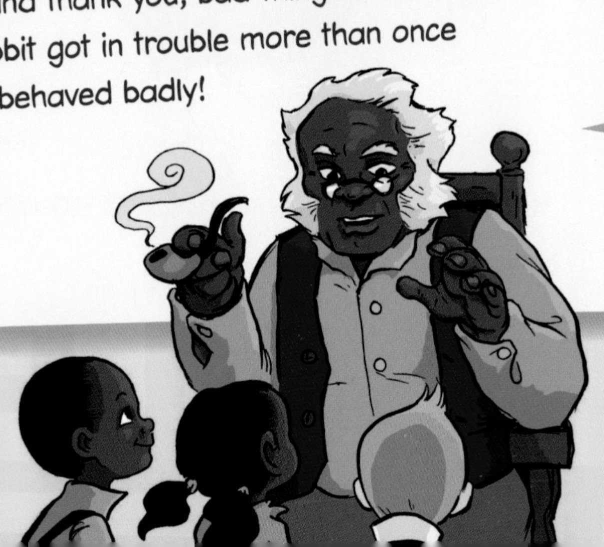